Walter Lorraine *wl* Books

Text copyright © 2002 by Harriet Ziefert
Illustrations copyright © 2002 by Todd McKie

www.houghtonmifflinbooks.com

Library of Congress Cataloging-in-Publication Data
Ziefert, Harriet.
Egad alligator! / story by Harriet Ziefert ; paintings by Todd McKie.
p. cm.
Summary: An innocent young alligator tries to make friends with various
animals, but they all run away, shouting, "Egad alligator!"
ISBN 0-618-14171-5
[1. Alligators—Fiction. 2. Animals—Fiction.] I. McKie, Todd, 1944-,
ill. II. Title.   PZ7.Z487 Ee 2002
[E]--dc21   2001004175

Printed in China for Harriet Ziefert, Inc.
1 3 5 7 9 10 8 6 4 2
HZI

EGAD ALLIGATOR!

by Harriet Ziefert   illustrated by Todd McKie

Houghton Mifflin Company Boston 2002

Walter Lorraine Books

Little Gator lived in a mangrove swamp with many other creatures.
"I'm tired," said Little Gator's brother.
"I'm gonna take a nap on the bank."

"Well, I'm not tired," said Little Gator,
"so I'm going exploring. See ya later, alligator!"

Little Gator said hello to a dragonfly,
who was hunting for insects.

He swam quietly through the water
until he spied something he had never seen before.

People!

In his friendliest voice he said,
"Nice day! How's the fishing?"

Egad

Little Gator moved along quickly . . .

until he came to a delicious-looking picnic.

Little Gator had never tried potato chips,
so he decided to help himself to some.

As he was about to grab a few, an arrow
flew right in front of his nose.

Little Gator ran for his life . . .

through prickly plants and thick foliage.

When he stopped running, Little Gator
found himself in a place where white herons
had built large nests high up in the trees.

Little Gator wanted to make friends, but the herons
thought he would steal their eggs. They flapped,
and squawked, and screeched.

Alone and tired, Little Gator walked onto
the edge of a field to rest and sun himself.
A softball game was about to begin.

Little Gator had a good view of the infield.
"Looks like fun," he said to himself.
"I bet I could catch that ball between my teeth."

Before Little Gator could say he wished
he could be on a team, a man in a uniform
tried to bop him over the head.

Little Gator ran as fast as his short legs
could carry him!

Now Little Gator wished he had never left home.
He was hungry, lost, and puzzled.

When he came to a big log, Little Gator thought
he'd take a little snooze, then continue on his way.

Little Gator swam for his life . . .

and did not stop to speak to anyone.

Finally, Little Gator was safely home.

"Where ya been?" his brother asked.

"Wanna go exploring?"